BY THE SAME AUTHOR

BEYOND
THE PAWPAW TREES

The Story of Anna Lavinia

by

PALMER BROWN

Drawings by the author

THE NEW YORK REVIEW
CHILDREN'S COLLECTION
New York

THIS IS A NEW YORK REVIEW BOOK
PUBLISHED BY THE NEW YORK REVIEW OF BOOKS
435 Hudson Street, New York, NY 10014
www.nyrb.com

Brown, Palmer.
Beyond the pawpaw trees : the story of Anna Lavinia / by Palmer
Brown ; illustrations by Palmer Brown.
p. cm. — (New York Review books children's collection)
Summary: Wondrous things happen when Anna Lavinia, a
young girl who lives in a distant house behind a grove of pawpaw
trees, sets off to travel to her aunt's house.
ISBN 978-1-59017-461-6 (alk. paper)
[1. Fantasy.] I. Title.
PZ7.B816647Be 2011
[Fic]—dc23

2011012574

ISBN 978-1-59017-461-6

Cover design by Louise Fili Ltd.

Printed in the United States on acid-free paper.
3 5 7 9 10 8 6 4 2

Contents

A map of Anna Lavinia's trip
follows page 75.

Chapter 1

Lavender Blue Days

BY THE very early morning light, Anna Lavinia was sitting at her bedroom window trying to thread a needle, and somehow it just would not thread. In getting a pair of clean stockings from her top bureau drawer, she had found two pieces of green silk ribbon

1

too short to be good for anything, and she wanted to sew them together before her mother rapped on the kitchen ceiling with a mopstick to let her know it was time for breakfast. Sewn together, the ribbons would be just long enough to make a bow for Strawberry, Anna Lavinia's ginger cat, who was still fast asleep at the foot of her bed.

But the needle simply would not thread. At first Anna Lavinia licked the end of the thread and twisted it, but that did not help. Then she cut the end of the thread and tried a fresh start, but that was no good either. Puzzled, she finally held the needle up to the light to see if there was something the matter with it. Perhaps there was a bit of lint in the eye. At once she realized what the trouble was. There was no use in even trying to thread a needle on such a day. Neither the needle nor the thread was to blame at all. It was the sky.

Raising the window shade all the way so that she might see better, Anna Lavinia looked out across the wide lawn, where the slanting sunlight winked from a thousand dewdrops on the grass. The air was filled with fine white thistledown which sifted slowly like silken snow onto the lawn, and the sky was a peculiar lavender blue color which Anna Lavinia knew meant the day would be topsy-turvy. Something unusual always happened on a day when the sky was lavender blue.

Once, on such a day, an excursion balloon passed overhead, bright with streamers and swinging a woven wicker basket filled with people looking out to smile and wave, and one of them had dropped a spyglass which fell

just beside the back porch. In falling the spy-glass had bent a bit, so that it did not work properly, but Anna Lavinia still found it useful in the attic to spy into the meadow beyond the garden wall.

On another lavender blue day, with almost as little wind as today, a prickly hedgehog blew over the garden wall, landing with a plump not two feet from the spot where Strawberry was taking his afternoon nap. The hedgehog seemed not half so much surprised as Anna Lavinia and Strawberry, and after a moment or two it unrolled itself, rattling its needles, and set about making a nest of moss halfway under a rock beside the well. There it would sleep most of the day, curled up like a pincushion, but in the evening it would creep out to nibble the young thistles which

sprang up all over the lawn shortly after a lavender blue day. Every morning Anna Lavinia could tell exactly where the hedgehog had been, because its nose left little round holes in the grass where it rooted the thistles out.

This morning, therefore, Anna Lavinia could not wait for her mother to tap on the ceiling to call her to breakfast. She was far too curious to see what the day would bring. There was always a chance, she thought, that on such a day her father, who had been away a very long time, might come home. Since she lived alone with her mother in a house so big that even her mother could not remember how many rooms there were, Anna Lavinia naturally missed her father very much.

So she put the bits of ribbon back in her bureau drawer beside the round pink stone and the green snail shell and the piece of speckled bird's egg with a brown and gold feather stuck to it which she was saving to ask her father about, and she went downstairs.

She was very careful to avoid the blue spots on the stair carpet and to step only on the pink ones, because that brought good luck. Her father had told her so once, at the same time that he had taught her how to shut her eyes and count three before opening them, in order to make sure of a thing.

Halfway downstairs, she was surprised to hear her mother singing in the kitchen:

> I held a sea shell to my ear,
>> Because they told me I would hear
> The magic song the mermaids sing,
>> The rush of waves along the shore.

The song was an old one which Anna Lavinia's mother had learned as a child, and those were all the words she could remember. What surprised Anna Lavinia, however, was that her mother was singing so early in the morning. It was only about half-past eight, and her mother usually never even spoke much until about ten o'clock, when she brewed the second pot of tea. It took something very special, like a lavender blue day, for her to break the habit.

Anna Lavinia remembered, as she sat down at her place at the kitchen table, that the last time her mother had sung at breakfast was the day when her mother had got a letter from Anna Lavinia's father, saying that he thought of coming home soon. That was a year ago last New Year's Day. At the time her mother had said, "Never believe what you see or hear. He will not come." And he had not come.

"Never believe what you see," was Anna Lavinia's mother's rule of life, which she used all the time to measure everything that happened. Anna Lavinia, however, somewhere in the back of her mind, remembered her father's rule of life, which he had given to Anna Lavinia just before he had gone away. That rule was: "Believe only what you see." Since Anna Lavinia liked rules that told you to do something rather than not to do something, she liked her father's rule better.

Once she tried to argue with her mother about the difference in the two rules, but her mother only said, very sharply, "Your father is chasing rainbows." Then she began to cry. Her mother almost always cried when she thought about Anna Lavinia's father, because she missed him so much, and Anna Lavinia, who hated to see her mother cry, was careful not to bring up the subject again. Still, she often thought to herself that it would be fun to be with her father and to chase rainbows with him. Though she had not seen him for more than two years, Anna Lavinia remembered clearly his bright red beard and the pocket microscope which he always carried to examine the motes in sunbeams. He

8

often promised to let Anna Lavinia look at them too, but somehow he never got around to it.

Anna Lavinia was thinking about these things at breakfast when her mother, who was rattling a kettle in the sink, turned to her and said, "I believe, Anna Lavinia, that it is about time for you to go and visit your father's sister."

Anna Lavinia was so excited that she stopped eating her oatmeal and left the spoon sticking straight up in the dish, where it popped open the melted lump of butter hidden there. For nearly two years her mother had been talking off and on about sending her on a visit to her Aunt Sophia Maria, but until today it was always one of those far away things parents always talk about but never get around to. Now that it was a fact, Anna Lavinia knew that it was a much better thing to happen on a lavender blue day than a spyglass. It was quite as good as a hedgehog. Indeed, it was the next best thing to having her father come home.

"And when you visit your Aunt Sophia Maria," her mother said, "you must not leave your spoon sticking straight up in your oatmeal dish, like a mast on a rowboat. Don't you hear, Anna Lavinia?"

Anna Lavinia heard, and she quickly took her spoon and put it beside her dish. Now that the butter had escaped, she did not feel much like eating the oatmeal anyway. But her mother did not scold her for not finishing her breakfast, because another of her rules was: "Do not eat unless you are hungry." Anna Lavinia did not think much of that rule either. "Eat because it is fun," was what her father had said. Once the butter had escaped, it wasn't fun any more.

Chapter 2

A Song from No Where

AFTER breakfast, Anna Lavinia went outdoors with Strawberry to watch the falling thistledown and to search out the trail of the hedgehog. Every morning she made a game of trailing where the hedgehog had been the night before by following the line of holes where it had eaten the tender thistles. But today she was far too excited to keep up with it very long, and instead she walked the whole way round her yard, thinking of her

Aunt Sophia Maria, whom she had never seen but whom she knew must be nice, because Anna Lavinia's mother told her that Aunt Sophia Maria had bright red hair just like Anna Lavinia's father's.

Anna Lavinia's house stood in the center of a square meadow surrounded by pawpaw trees, and beyond the pawpaw trees was a high brick wall with only one small iron gate opening onto the road to the village. As she walked beneath the trees, Anna Lavinia knocked at the branches now and then with a stick to see if the pawpaws were ripe. Those that fell she heaped together in little piles to be taken into the house later.

The pawpaws were good for making pawpaw jelly, which Anna Lavinia's mother made all the time. This kept them very busy, for the pawpaws ripened almost faster than they could gather them, and as soon as they had finished making one batch of jelly, it was time to start in on another. It seemed to Anna Lavinia that she was always picking pawpaws

13

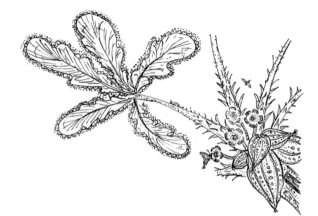

or stirring jelly or writing out labels and pasting them on the jars. She really did not see why they bothered to put labels on the jars, since they could always tell by the color that it was pawpaw jelly. Because they never could eat all the jelly that they made, the pantry outside the kitchen was filled to the ceiling with jelly jars. All the light that came through the pantry windows was pale pink pawpaw color, and about a year ago they gave up trying to go in or out the kitchen door, because the jelly jars were too much in the way. So they went in and out the front door to fetch water from the well, which was just beside the back porch.

The rosy brick wall around the meadow beyond the pawpaw trees was not really good for anything, because it was too high to climb over and too narrow to walk along the top of. Anna Lavinia's mother said that there was nothing to see on the other side anyway, and since they had no neighbors nor any reason to go anywhere, maybe she was right. Certainly there was very little to see out the iron gate except the dusty road and sometimes a cart of vegetables passing down it on the way to the nearest village or, once a week, the man who brought groceries from the village, leaving them just at the iron gate and reading the grocery list which Anna Lavinia's mother had her write out on a little blackboard tied there.

Nevertheless, especially on lavender blue days like today, Anna Lavinia could not help thinking that the world beyond the pawpaw trees and the brick wall must be a very wonderful place, full of strange things. She knew, at least, that the field beyond the wall, which was as far as she could see from the attic with the bent spyglass, was filled with buttercups that were pink instead of yellow as were the ones in her garden. Surely a world where buttercups grew pink and hedgehogs blew over garden walls was a marvelous world where almost anything could happen.

Going back to the house, Anna Lavinia stopped by the well to peep in on the hedgehog. In the nest of moss and thistledown beneath its stone, the hedgehog seemed to be sleeping as soundly as a pincushion. Half to herself, because she knew that animals cannot talk, Anna Lavinia whispered, "What sort of a world is it out there? You ought to know." The hedgehog squirmed in its sleep, perhaps only because a bit of thistledown was tickling its nose, yet Anna Lavinia was almost certain, though not quite sure, that the hedgehog opened one eye and winked at her. In one of the pawpaw trees a dove called: "Who? who? who? Tell me," and beyond the wall another dove answered: "You, you, you! Tell me." As she went into the house, Anna Lavinia thought it was a good sign.

After lunch, while her mother was peeling pawpaws, Anna Lavinia went up to the attic to study. Although she was old enough to go to school, her mother had never troubled to send her. When the time had come for her to go, her mother thought about it for an hour or so and decided not to send her.

"It is really too far to the village," her mother had said. "Besides, there is nothing for you to learn there except reading and writing and arithmetic, and you can pick that up around the house if you really want to." When her mother told Anna Lavinia that she certainly could not take Strawberry with her if she went to school, she was just as glad not to go.

Therefore Anna Lavinia taught herself reading and writing, while her mother helped her some with the arithmetic, using jars of pawpaw jelly for examples. This worked out pretty well on addition and multiplication, but since the pawpaw jars never got less, Anna Lavinia had more trouble with subtraction and division. Learning fractions was especially a nuisance, because it usually meant eating a half or a third of a jar of jelly to make the problems come out even.

The writing was easy, though. Filling out the grocery list on the little blackboard by the gate gave Anna Lavinia lots of practice. Sometimes she used colored chalk, ordering butter with yellow and apples with red. Other times she just drew little pictures of the things they needed, but her mother finally asked her to be sure to write as well, for once the man brought a bag of salt instead of sugar, right in the midst of jelly-making time.

As for reading, the attic was full of interesting books which belonged to Anna Lavinia's father, telling about strange countries and undiscovered islands. Anna Lavinia would read for hours at a time, lying on the

floor in the attic, with a book placed just so
the pages were lighted by the sunshine which
came through an opening where the shingles
in the roof were missing. As she turned the
pages, Strawberry would play with the silk
ribbons which hung from the books for book-
marks, and the mice, which he never bothered
to catch, would come out from their boxes
and trunks to spy on them.

One of Anna Lavinia's favorite books,
which she was reading today, was the *Geography of the Desert.* It told all about the
Arabs who lived in the desert and the oases
where they made their homes, and it had
pictures in color of all the strange flowers that
bloom in the desert when it rains, if it rains.
Her mother said she did not believe a word
of this book because it was her father's, and
that was another reason Anna Lavinia liked

it, since her father had made a little "X" on all the pictures of flowers he had actually seen, and once or twice he had written at the bottom of the page: "It is even prettier than the picture."

The book Anna Lavinia liked the very best of all was Mrs. Tetterbrace's *Songs from Nowhere*. Anna Lavinia could never be certain whether "Nowhere" meant "No where" or "Now here," but she learned all the songs by heart. It was a lucky thing that she learned them, because one day the book was missing, and ever afterwards she could not find it. It happened the very day after her mother was angry with her for dropping pawpaw pits in the well to hear the echo. When Anna Lavinia was punished by being locked in the big cupboard with the mops and brooms, she sang Mrs. Tetterbrace's song, "Touch Me Not," over and over again through the keyhole until her mother let her out. First she had to promise never to sing it any more. And the next day the book was missing.

Sometimes, however, like today, when she was alone with Strawberry, she would whisper the song softly to herself, for she had not promised not to whisper it, and Strawberry would put his paws before his eyes, pretending to cry, as Anna Lavinia whispered:

> Touch me not, touch me not!
> Kiss me, I'll cry.
> There's nothing the matter,
> But a tear in my eye.

> I'll stand in the corner,
> I'll sulk in the gloom,
> And if I were able,
> I'd smash the whole room!

A Song from No Where

Anna Lavinia had just finished whispering the song when her mother rattled open the attic door and called her. Popping shut the *Geography of the Desert*, Anna Lavinia jumped to her feet. "I wasn't singing," she said.

"It doesn't matter what you were doing, dear," her mother answered. "Bring down the old blue carpetbag with the red roses on it. I want you to help me pack your things."

After turning the carpetbag upside down first to make sure that there were no mice in it, Anna Lavinia hurried downstairs with it, thinking that this was the finest lavender blue day ever.

Chapter 3

Keys Large and Small

THE next morning before it was quite light, Anna Lavinia woke up in a hurry when her mother tapped the mopstick against the kitchen ceiling. There was no time to get out of bed little by little, as she usually did in order to get her feet used to the cold floor. After quickly tucking back the coverlet over

Strawberry, who seemed a little grumpy because she let the window shades rattle up, Anna Lavinia put on her freshly ironed best blue dress and smoothed the ribbons on her flowered straw hat. The carpetbag was all packed beside her bed, and as she was putting on her shoes, her mother bustled into the room to add six jars of pawpaw jelly and a hot-water bottle in case it was cold at Aunt Sophia Maria's house. After breakfast, as her mother was wrapping sandwiches for her to eat on the train, Anna Lavinia ran upstairs to say good-bye to Strawberry.

She could not find him anywhere, although she even looked in her bottom bureau drawer, which she always left a little open so that he might sleep there when he did not wish to be disturbed. She would have looked in the attic too, but her mother called up to her just then, "Anna Lavinia, come!"

Since three words from her mother this early in the morning were as important as thirty words later in the day, Anna Lavinia picked up her carpetbag and carried it down to the front door where her mother stood waiting. In one hand her mother held a potted gardenia bush for Anna Lavinia to take to her Aunt Sophia Maria, and in the other hand she twirled by its purple tassel Anna Lavinia's favorite plum-colored umbrella with the gold handle. It made Anna Lavinia feel quite grown-up to know that she was being trusted with that umbrella, which was very old, although the silk was good as new.

Taking a big iron key, her mother unlocked
the gate while Anna Lavinia wrote "Cream
for Strawberry" on the blackboard in case her
mother might forget. Then, just as the sun
came up before them, Anna Lavinia stepped
out onto the dusty road for the first time in her
life. With each step, the dust rose up in little
puffs behind her, and it was not at all like the
grass to walk on. When the gate clicked behind them, Anna Lavinia looked back to see
the hedgehog curiously watching her. This
time she was sure that it winked at her as it
turned and scuttled towards its nest. To Anna
Lavinia the sky seemed very wide without the
brick wall to cut off the view, and far in front
of her, at the foot of a gently sloping hill, she
could see the village where she was to take
the train.

She and her mother had not walked more
than a mile or so, passing the field full of
pink buttercups, when a brightly painted

vegetable cart creaked up to them. The driver stopped his horse and asked them if they wanted to ride along to the village with him. Although Anna Lavinia's mother did not say anything because it was too early in the morning, she nevertheless climbed up into the cart quickly enough, sitting down on a basket of broad beans. The man then helped Anna Lavinia up with her carpetbag, and she chose a basket of purple cabbages to sit on, more because they were pretty than comfortable.

"Are you strangers here?" the man asked, when they were on their way again.

Anna Lavinia's mother still did not speak, since she was busy thinking about her second pot of tea, so Anna Lavinia answered, telling the man where they lived.

The vegetable cart man looked at them both for a long time, pushing his tattered straw hat back on his head as if he were trying to remember something, but he did not ask any more questions all the way to the village. When they arrived at the railroad station, however, while Anna Lavinia's mother was inside buying a ticket for her, the man smiled at Anna Lavinia and said, "I think I met your father once. He wouldn't happen to have red hair like you, would he?"

Anna Lavinia was thrilled. "And a red beard," she said.

"I thought there was something familiar about your face," the man said. "I picked your father up in a thunderstorm about a year ago, and he rode with me a couple of miles.

Then a strange thing happened. All at once the rain stopped and the sun came out, turning the sky a peculiar blue color."

"Lavender blue?" Anna Lavinia interrupted.

"I suppose you could call it that," the vegetable man answered. "Anyway," he continued, "the moment the rain stopped, there was a great double rainbow behind us, straddling the sky like a giant horseshoe. Your father took one look at the rainbow and cried out, 'A double one!' Then he leaped out of the cart without another word, and ran back down the road the way we had just come."

"My father chases rainbows," Anna Lavinia explained. She did not want the man to think her father acted without reason.

"I figured that was what it was," the vegetable cart man said. "But your father was in such a hurry that he forgot something." At this he went over to his horse and took from around its neck a faded blue string with a silver key tied to it. "Take this," he said to

Anna Lavinia, "and give it back to your
father."

Before Anna Lavinia could say that she
did not know where her father was, the cart
had gone and her mother was calling her. So
she carefully put the key in her pocket and
for the moment forgot all about it.

When she sat down on the painted green
bench to wait for the train, her mother gave
her the ticket and said, "Anna Lavinia, it
may be some time before the train gets here,
and I cannot wait. All you have to do when
it comes is to get on. I must get busy with the
jelly, and it just occurred to me that perhaps
I had better write your Aunt Sophia Maria
to tell her that I am sending you." With that
she kissed Anna Lavinia and walked back up
the road.

Anna Lavinia watched her mother disappear up the road, knowing perfectly well that she was really hurrying so that she might brew the second pot of tea by ten o'clock. Only after she was out of sight did Anna Lavinia remember that she had forgotten to tell her mother about the key, but it was too late now. She put her hand in her pocket to make sure that it was still there. Now that her mother was gone, it made her feel a little less alone to have something belonging to her father, and for a long time she held it tightly in her fist.

Chapter 4

Taste of Peppermint

FINALLY the train came. Anna Lavinia was surprised to see that there was only the engine and one coach, faded rose color with the paint peeling off and the gilt turning green. She had always thought of trains as much longer, with lots of steam and noise and whistles blowing. Yet this train coasted into the station with a sort of soft sighing wheeze, as if it were weary, and there was hardly any steam at all. Even the bell rang slowly, with a thin, tired tinkle, and you had to listen twice before you heard it.

The engineer, who was also the conductor, climbed down from the rattling engine, wearing an old navy-blue uniform with red piping and brass buttons and a little cap with a drooping visor which once had been red, but now was covered with coal dust. He helped Anna Lavinia into the coach, where all the seats were covered with blue and green striped velvet to match the blue and green striped velvet curtains at the windows. The engineer led Anna Lavinia to a seat facing the only other passenger on the train. This was an immensely fat woman in a purple-flowered silk dress, fast asleep, with a dozen packages piled high on the seat beside her.

After taking Anna Lavinia's ticket, the engineer said to her, "This will be a long trip for you. I see you are going all the way." As he spoke, the ends of his drooping mustache bobbed up and down.

Anna Lavinia said, "Yes," in a very small voice, but she did not have any idea what he meant by all the way. She had looked at her

ticket carefully, and it was only a square piece
of yellow pasteboard with no printing on it.
She supposed the engineer could tell by the
color of the ticket where she was going.

The engineer went ahead to start up the
train again, and almost at once Anna Lavinia
saw the town fly past and the trees and farms
and meadows whirl away in the distance.
Just when she was beginning to get a good
look at something, it was gone. Things that
were close to the train moved much faster
than things further away, so that what was
just outside the window was blurred and very
hard to see.

After a while the fat woman woke up and yawned tremendously several times. She smiled at Anna Lavinia pleasantly, so Anna Lavinia smiled back. Once she had got used to the fat woman's size, Anna Lavinia began to find her quite nice.

"A train always makes me sleepy," the fat woman said. "Doesn't it you?"

Anna Lavinia, taking off her hat and putting it on the seat beside her, said, no, she didn't think so, at least not yet, but she did wonder why the scenery just outside the window moved so much faster.

"I had not noticed," the fat woman replied, and then looked to see. "It must be because it is closer. Things that are closer are always harder to understand. If someone asks you if you like peppermints, for instance, you know what they taste like of course, and you take one. But if you have a peppermint in your mouth and try to think how it tastes, that is much harder. You can only say that it is sort of sweet and sort of sharp, with a striped taste."

Anna Lavinia thought that a striped taste described peppermint pretty well, and if she were ordering peppermints on her blackboard, striped letters would be just the thing, but she began to understand what the fat woman meant. Things close at hand were puzzling. Only when today was rolled up in a little ball and became yesterday could you really begin to understand it.

Talking of peppermints evidently made the fat woman hungry, for she opened one of her many packages and took out about twenty little chicken sandwiches, all cut round with no crust on the bread. She offered them to Anna Lavinia, who, seeing they would be fun to eat, said she would take some, just to keep the fat woman company.

"There is no better reason for eating," the fat woman said. "I always eat to keep someone company, or else find someone to keep company with me when I eat."

37

When they had eaten all the sandwiches, the fat woman opened another package which was full of iced cakes, each a different color, with birds and flowers and sugar angels on the top. Anna Lavinia kept the fat woman company eating them too, and she had to try a dozen different ones, each better than the last.

The fat woman told Anna Lavinia that she spent most of her time making tea cosies to put over teapots to keep them warm. Once a month she took all that she had made to the next town to sell them, and that was what she was doing today. Anna Lavinia had never seen a tea cosy, so the fat woman opened one of her packages and took out a pink one with blue forget-me-nots sewn round the edge.

"You may keep it, if you like," she said to Anna Lavinia. "You never know when you might need a tea cosy."

Anna Lavinia thanked her and opened the blue carpetbag to put the tea cosy in. When she opened it, she was delighted to see Strawberry there, sound asleep on top of the six jars of pawpaw jelly.

Strawberry opened his eyes and leaped out of the carpetbag into Anna Lavinia's lap, purring so loudly that she could hardly hear the rumbling of the train. Anna Lavinia took him in her arms and hugged him, smoothing his whiskers, which were a little bent from being shut in the carpetbag.

The fat woman stared at Strawberry a moment without being able to speak. Then she gave a little cry—a very little cry for so large a person—and, looking as if she might faint, she said, "Put him away! Put him away! Please!"

As quickly as she could, Anna Lavinia pushed Strawberry back into the carpetbag and shut it tight, first taking out a jar of pawpaw jelly to make more room for Strawberry's whiskers.

The fat woman sighed, fanning her face with an empty paper bag. "I am sorry to have shouted at you that way," she said, "but I was born with a horror of all cats. They make me turn green." And indeed, Anna Lavinia noticed, she was quite green.

The fat woman continued, "Thank you for putting him away so promptly. Mind you, I make no reflection on your cat. He is a beautiful color, like raspberry-fluff, which is my favorite dessert on Tuesdays. Is that something to eat you have there?"

Anna Lavinia gave the fat woman the jar of pawpaw jelly, which she had to taste right away, because she had never tasted pawpaw jelly before. "I think it is wonderful," she exclaimed, when she had finished the whole jar, eating it with a small silver spoon from her handbag. Anna Lavinia saw that she was beginning to get her color back again.

"Did you make the jelly yourself?" the fat woman asked.

Anna Lavinia explained to her how she and

her mother made the jelly, and how they had so many jars of it that they did not know where to put them next. The fat woman listened carefully, and when Anna Lavinia had finished telling her about the pantry being so full of jelly jars that they could not use the back door, the fat woman began to laugh so heartily that all her packages bounced up and down on the seat. Gradually Anna Lavinia began to laugh too, because it was catching,

and she realized for the first time that not being able to use the back door was a little foolish.

"You know," the fat woman said, wiping the tears of laughter from her eyes with the tiniest handkerchief Anna Lavinia had ever seen, "that is exactly what happened with me and my tea cosies. Then, one day, a little boy who lives down the road and sometimes comes over to keep me company around tea time, said to me that I ought to sell the cosies. So I do. And when you get home, be sure to tell your mother to sell the pawpaw jelly. I'm sure lots of people would buy it and, of course, then you'd be able to use the back door again."

Anna Lavinia thought that this was a very good idea. The more she thought of it, the more she wondered why she had not thought of it herself.

It was beginning to rain now, and they could not see anything except the fat rain-drops sliding down the windowpane, so the fat woman suggested that they sing songs to pass the time. With all the *Songs from Nowhere* to choose from, Anna Lavinia was prepared to sing for hours. Therefore she began with Mrs. Tetterbrace's song about the greedy boy:

Taste of Peppermint

Dimpled George, he loved to gorge
    Upon his mother's mincemeat pie.
She feared the worst, and vowed he'd burst,
    George laughed and said, "Just let me try!"

And since she was simple, she'd kiss either
        dimple,
    Amazed at an answer so speedy.
Some risk, true, she took, but she so loved to
        cook,
    For George was her joy——even greedy.

Such mother's love would spoil a dove,
    And she grew lean while George grew
        fatter.
His fate is plain, though without pain,
    But, oh! the pantry! What a splatter!

The fat woman seemed to enjoy the song
all the way to the last line, for she tapped her
foot to the tune, but when Anna Lavinia was
done, the fat woman frowned and said that
she did not think the song was very amusing,

and she had not tapped her foot during the last line, which is where you should stamp your foot the most. The fat woman said she liked the song she was going to sing much better, but first she must take a deep breath, because it had to be sung all at once. Then, pretending that the empty pawpaw jelly jar was a kettle and the little silver spoon a soup ladle, the fat woman stirred the spoon round and round the jelly jar as she sang:

Oh! Put on the kettle and stew me a goose,
When it is done, boil some rice in the juice.
Serve it with celery, carrots and peas.
Butter it! Salt it! Pepper it! Please.
Take a potato and half a tomato.
Hurry up! Hurry up! Oh, I can't wait, oh!

Anna Lavinia waited for more, but that seemed to be all there was to the song. It reminded her, however, of the song about the dappled duck, which she sang next:

44

Taste of Peppermint

A dappled duck with silver feet
Stood crying by a muddy street.
"I will not," wept the dappled duck,
"Soil silver feet with marshy muck."

From all the news that I can get,
That dappled duck is standing yet,
His feathers wet with dappled tears,
His heart grown faint with duckish fears.

Too proud to wet his silver feet
By marching through a muddy street,
The dappled duck will learn too late:
They starve who won't accept their fate.

It always made Anna Lavinia a little sad to
sing this song, and she looked over at the fat
woman to see whether she felt that way too,
but she had fallen asleep again, with the
empty pawpaw jelly jar jiggling in her lap
and the silver spoon tinkling in it as the train
rattled forward through the brightening afternoon.

Chapter 5

Towards the Horizon

WHEN Anna Lavinia was quite sure that the fat woman was sleeping soundly, she opened her carpetbag just a crack to see if Strawberry was comfortable, and he was. Then she took out another jar of pawpaw jelly and walked up to the front of the coach, where she could see the engineer eating his lunch of brown bread and sausages. He was very grateful to have the pawpaw jelly, and he took Anna Lavinia up into the engine where she could see the tracks stretching way out in front of the train. The further away the tracks were, the closer together they ran, until finally there was no space between them at all, and they were just a point at the very edge of the sky.

Anna Lavinia was troubled. "What will happen," she asked, "when we reach the place where the tracks run together?"

The engineer at first laughed at the question, and Anna Lavinia wondered if perhaps she had said something foolish. Then he became serious, and his mustache drooped. "We will just have to wait and see," he said, admitting that he had never been on this part of the track before. He supposed that the wheels of the train would push the tracks apart, or else that the tracks would push the wheels together. Anna Lavinia had to be satisfied with that, though it really was no answer at all.

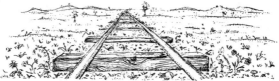

The train was now chugging slowly up a steep hill. The engineer told Anna Lavinia that when they reached the top they would stop, and that she had better go and wake the fat woman, because that was where the fat woman was getting off. By the time she went back to wake her, the fat woman was already yawning and gathering her packages together.

"I can always tell when we are nearly there," she said to Anna Lavinia, "because this particular hill is so steep that it is hard for me to keep from rolling out of the seat."

The hill was in fact so steep that every once in a while the train slipped back with a screeching sound, and twice the fat woman's packages all rolled onto the floor. Anna Lavinia held her breath each time the train skidded, and she reached into her pocket to touch the silver key for good luck. At last the train reached the top of the hill, where it stopped, with the engine leaning a little down one side and the coach leaning a little back down the other.

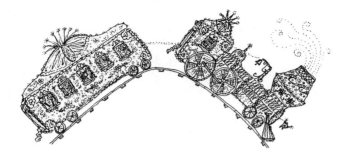

As the fat woman stepped down from the train, she said good-bye to Anna Lavinia and told her to be sure to let Strawberry out of the carpetbag, since no one else seemed to be getting on the train. Anna Lavinia was sorry to see her go. The engineer climbed down from the engine to help the fat woman put her bundles on a bench. In the meantime Anna Lavinia took Strawberry out of the carpetbag, but she made him stay away from the window as long as the fat woman was watching. When the train began to move again, Anna Lavinia leaned out of the window to wave to the fat woman. Standing on the platform beside her, so surprised that he could not move, was the engineer with his mouth wide open and his mustache all a-droop, watching his train roll down the hill away from him.

49

The train clattered down the hillside and up and down another hill or two so quickly that Anna Lavinia did not even have time to wonder what was going to happen next. For a little while she thought that she was going to cry, until she considered it and could not see what there was to cry about. Nothing she had ever read told her what to do on a train without an engineer. Perhaps, she finally decided, it was not so very unusual after all.

Soon the train had passed through the hilly country and began traveling slowly through a flat land without trees or houses or anything to see. Anna Lavinia discovered that the fat woman had left behind one of her packages. She knew it was not right to open up other people's things, but she was curious to know what was in it. Putting the package on the edge of the seat, she let the string that tied it hang over the edge, where it wiggled with the movement of the train. Very soon Strawberry began to play with the string, and in no time at all the package was open.

Anna Lavinia scolded Strawberry, because it was the right thing to do, but she was not really angry with him. Once the string was untied, there could be no harm in seeing what was in the package. It turned out that the package had in it six radishes and a bunch of green onions, twelve roast beef sandwiches, two cherry tarts, and one medium-sized apple-sauce cake with whole almonds stuck all over in the icing, so that the cake looked like a hedgehog. At the bottom of it all was a note from the fat woman, written on lavender note paper and reading: "I am leaving you this, because I know you did not count on having to feed your nice cat on the train."

Anna Lavinia felt much better about having opened the package, and she could not help thinking how kind it was of the fat woman to remember Strawberry when the sight of a cat made her turn green. Strawberry

felt better too when he had eaten most of the sandwiches, although he would not touch the green onions, which Anna Lavinia finally tucked out of the way under one of the seats.

Gradually it began to get dark. The train seemed to be getting along quite well without the engineer, and Anna Lavinia hardly ever thought about being alone any more. When the train finally went into a long tunnel, there was nothing for Anna Lavinia to do but to curl up on the seat beside Strawberry and sing herself to sleep with the song about the garden, sung in time to the clumping of the wheels:

I had a little fig tree,
    Drooping down with figs,
My neighbor came and picked them,
    And fed them to his pigs.

I had a little arbor,
    Grapes on every stem,
He stole into my garden,
    And gathered all of them.

53

I had a little berry bush,
  Rosy-red with fruit,
My neighbor crammed his basket,
  And ran off with the loot.

I had a little melon vine,
  With melons honey-sweet,
He popped them in a burlap bag,
  And fled in stocking feet.

I had a little quince tree,
  With quinces hard as stone,
And do you know? My neighbor came,
  But left that tree alone.

Now, though I love my neighbor,
  Since it is wrong to hate,
I think that I must put a lock
  Upon my garden gate.

For there's a sort of neighbor
  Whom nothing else convinces,
Except large locks on garden gates,
  Or gardens full of quinces.

In the morning, Anna Lavinia awoke to
find that the train was winding back and forth
slowly through a wild forest where the trees
were so tall and so thickly tangled with morn-
ing-glories and wild grape vines that the sunlight could not get all the way through, but
stopped about halfway down the mossy trunks.
Fireflies twinkled in the darkness below,
while birds were singing in the sunny tree-
tops. Wide branches covered with orange
mushrooms reached across the narrow space
cleared for the train to pass through, and
sometimes the shaggy branches hung so low
that the train could hardly brush past them.

Anna Lavinia climbed up in the engine to look ahead along the tracks, which were almost covered with sweet-smelling pine needles. Today there was no denying that the tracks were much closer together than yesterday. It was nice to see this happening, even though the train seemed to be creaking much more than usual, because Anna Lavinia now knew that sometime soon the tracks would have to meet and the train would not go any further.

That is exactly what happened. Anna Lavinia and Strawberry were eating part of the fat woman's applesauce cake for breakfast when the train shot out of the forest into dazzling daylight and began to climb the steepest hill yet. Going up into the engine again, Anna Lavinia and Strawberry peered ahead, squinting in the sunshine. There, just a little below the top of the hill, they saw that the tracks ended, coming together in a sharp point in the center of a clump of pink buttercups.

As the train neared the end of the tracks, there was a lot of squeaking in the wheels. The train stopped. All the steam hissed out of the engine, and it was so quiet that Anna Lavinia could hear the bees buzzing among the pink buttercups. She ran back to the coach and put on her hat. Then she picked up her blue carpetbag with the red roses on it and her plum-colored umbrella with the gold handle and the gardenia bush, and she and Strawberry hurried off the train as quickly as they could for fear it might roll back down the hill. There was no need to worry about that, however. All the wheels of the engine were pushed together as tight as a pawpaw jelly sandwich. It did not look as though the train would ever be able to run again.

Chapter 6

A Pasha and a Parrot

ANNA LAVINIA looked around her, bewildered. There was no railroad station. There were no houses. There was not even a road. The only thing in sight was a large sign in very small letters, reading, "END OF THE LINE," but that did not help very much, and Anna Lavinia had not the slightest idea where to go next. The best thing to do, she finally decided, was to continue on up to the top of the hill to see what was on the other side. The hill was steep and covered with slippery stones, which made it hard to climb, and the carpetbag and the gardenia bush kept getting heavier and heavier. At last Anna Lavinia reached the very top and looked ahead.

There was no other side to the hill. The ground dropped straight down in a steep cliff. It seemed a mile or so to the bottom, and it made Anna Lavinia quite dizzy to look. At the bottom there was nothing but sandy desert, except in the distance she could just make out that there was a town with a wall around it. The town had tall pink and white towers with round tops like onions, and there were palm trees growing over the walls, just like the pictures Anna Lavinia had studied in her *Geography of the Desert.*

If only she could get down to the desert, Anna Lavinia thought, she could easily walk to the town. But as far as she could see in either direction the cliff was far too steep to climb down. Here and there a twisted bush or stunted tree thrust out from a crack in the cliff, but they all looked too spindly to hang onto. She was really no closer to the desert, she thought, than when she was in her attic just reading about it. Once or twice she peered over the edge, and each time a hot blast of air from the desert below blew in her face. Discouraged, she finally sat on the edge of the cliff, letting her feet hang over just a little bit in the warm air. It was heartbreaking, she felt, to have come all this way and to be so near, and yet not be able to go any further. A little angrily, Anna Lavinia picked up a small stone and threw it over the edge.

Now a curious thing happened. The stone did not fall right away. It bobbed and bounced in the hot air for a long time, then slowly began to sink down towards the desert. Anna Lavinia thought of her mother's advice, "Never believe what you see," and she was tempted to follow it. Stones certainly never acted that way at home. Anna Lavinia looked at one closely. It seemed quite ordinary, but when she tossed it over the edge it did the same thing. She thought she would try something else, because perhaps only stones acted that way, so she opened her carpetbag and found the fat woman's tea cosy and tossed it out. The tea cosy was so light that it would

not go down at all. A jar of pawpaw jelly
went down pretty well, a little slower than
the stones.

Strawberry, who had been watching the tea cosy whirling in the air just over the edge of the cliff, reached out to catch it with one of his paws, and, sliding on a flat stone, slipped over the edge. Anna Lavinia held her breath as she watched him clawing at the air a couple of feet below the edge. Then he curled up in a tight ball, looking exactly like the hedgehog the day it had blown over the garden wall, and very slowly Strawberry slipped out of sight, seeming not to mind it a bit.

Anna Lavinia came to a great decision. There was nothing else to do but follow Strawberry. First she pushed the carpetbag over the edge. Next she started the gardenia bush on its way, making sure that it was right side up. Finally, just to be on the safe side, she opened her umbrella and reached into her pocket to squeeze the silver key for good luck. Then she took a deep breath and stepped off into the air.

Going down was not bad at all. Sometimes the wind blew her back up a few feet, and she

would have to close the umbrella a bit to keep
going in the right direction, but generally she
went down pretty fast. How she wished the
people in the excursion balloon might have
seen her now! Or, for that matter, the hedgehog with his sly winking. She soon passed the
jar of pawpaw jelly and the gardenia bush,
which she straightened in passing. When she
reached Strawberry, she stretched out her
hand and caught him. After that they went
down a little faster.

The carpetbag reached the bottom first. Anna Lavinia landed next, then the gardenia bush, and finally the jar of pawpaw jelly. The tea cosy never did come down. Anna Lavinia waited for it about ten minutes, because the fat woman had said that you never know when you might need a tea cosy, but at last she had to give up.

Gathering her things together, Anna Lavinia commenced walking towards the strange walled town, which appeared to be much further away than it had looked from the top of the cliff. Strawberry walked beside her, and because the sand was hot, at every step he shook his paws to cool them.

At the gate of the town, Anna Lavinia put down her carpetbag and rapped at the great

carved wooden door six or seven times. When no one answered, she pushed the door as hard as she could, and it swung open just far enough for her to squeeze through. Before her was a crooked street with shops along both sides, and in front of the shops under the striped awnings people were sitting asleep on the ground or on huge cushions of embroidered silk and leather. They all looked like the Arabs in her geography book, since they wore twisted turbans and a sort of nightgown with tasseled sashes and bright leather shoes with curled toes. Anna Lavinia remembered that Arabs sleep most of the time during the heat of the day, and after her long journey across the sun-baked sand she understood why. There was nothing to do until they woke up, so she sat down in the shade of a palm tree and, after pouring the sand from her shoes, she took a nap too.

A noise of people talking around her soon awakened her. She saw the Arabs standing about her in a circle, jabbering to themselves.

Some of the women were opening and shutting her umbrella to see how it worked and others were sniffing the roses on her carpetbag or petting Strawberry, who was delighted with the attention. When they saw that Anna Lavinia was awake, they all began shouting, "Salaam-alaam-alaam-alaam-alaam-alaam!"

"I believe," Anna Lavinia said, "that what you are saying means hello. But I think we would understand each other a little better if you would speak English."

After that they all spoke English. They asked her where she came from and what she wanted there. When she pointed to the cliff in the distance and said she came from there, they laughed, rolling on the ground, and said it was not possible. No one ever came down the cliff. No one could. Anna Lavinia tried to explain just how she came down the cliff, but the Arabs were all laughing so much that they would not listen, and Anna Lavinia began to think that speaking English did not really help very much, if people would not believe what they saw or heard.

A very old man crooked his skinny finger at her and squeaked, "She is dizzy from the sand and sunlight. Give her a glass of buttermilk and she will talk more sensibly."

Someone ran into one of the shops to get the buttermilk, but Anna Lavinia, who hated buttermilk and who remembered that Arabs keep it in oily leather bottles, said, "Thank you. Could I, please, have water instead? I think the buttermilk may be a little rich for me, though my cat would love some, I'm sure."

They gave her the water, although the old man with the skinny finger said it would not help so much as buttermilk, and next he told her that she must be taken to the Pasha, who would decide what to do about her.

They led her down the crooked street, past shops filled with shoes with curled toes and pointed saddles for camels and huge baskets of figs and dates and prickly pears, until they came to the Pasha's pink marble palace and went in. The Pasha was a very fat Arab wearing an embroidered green vest and gold pantaloons with a red silk sash. He was sitting on a blue satin pillow, fast asleep, with a jeweled curved sword at his side. While Anna Lavinia was waiting politely for him to finish his nap, she walked all around the border of the Oriental rug, stepping only on the pink parts of the pattern for good luck.

When the Pasha was thoroughly awake and had got over the surprise of seeing Anna

Lavinia and Strawberry tiptoeing round the edge of his rug, he said that he was pleased to have her visit him and that he would help her to find her aunt if he could. No one had ever heard of her Aunt Sophia Maria, however. The Pasha supposed that she must live further out in the desert. He promised to give Anna Lavinia a camel to make it easier to travel. First, however, she must break bread with him.

Breaking bread was quite agreeable with Anna Lavinia, and she knew that once the bread had been broken, she and the Pasha would be friends, for that was an Arab custom. Yet she was hardly prepared for the strange thin loaf of round black bread which the Pasha picked up from a silver tray and held out to her. Anna Lavinia gripped her side of the loaf with both hands and pulled, while the Pasha twisted at the other end.

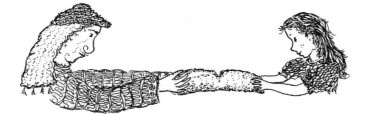

After a great deal of tugging, the bread was finally broken. It had a dry, rather musty taste, and Anna Lavinia thought it scarcely worth all that trouble.

"Very few people ever come here," the Pasha said with a yawn when the bread had been broken. "It is a little out of the way. Once in a while someone comes to study the local color. What do you think of the local color?"

"It is quite nice," Anna Lavinia said, just to be polite. The local color was mostly pale pink, and too much like pawpaw jelly to suit her. But the nightgowns with sashes and the shoes with curled toes made up for it.

The Pasha wanted to see what was in Anna Lavinia's carpetbag, and he asked her to take everything out of it.

"What is this?" he asked, holding up the hot-water bottle.

"It is a hot-water bottle," Anna Lavinia answered.

The Pasha took out the cork and turned the

bottle upside down. He looked disappointed.
"There is no hot water in it."

Anna Lavinia tried hard not to laugh.
"You must put the hot water in."

The Pasha clapped his hands three times and a servant came in with a huge copper kettle of boiling water which the Pasha poured into the hot-water bottle with a golden ladle. "Now what do you do with it?" he asked.

Anna Lavinia explained that you put it under your feet at night to keep them warm, but the Pasha could not understand this at all.

"My feet are always warm here," he complained. "I wish I could keep them cool."

Anna Lavinia considered this. "I guess you could put ice water in the hot-water bottle," she suggested.

"But it wouldn't be a hot-water bottle any more then, would it?" asked the Pasha.

It had never occurred to Anna Lavinia that a thing could stop being what it was. "I suppose not," she answered. "But there's no harm in calling it whatever you like, and if you want to, you may keep it."

The Pasha beamed. "That's cold comfort, indeed!" he said.

Anna Lavinia also gave him a jar of paw-paw jelly and the rest of the fat woman's applesauce cake, which by now was a little stale anyway. At any rate, it could not be worse than the Pasha's bread. The Pasha thanked her for her presents, and he clapped his hands three times again. A man led in a small camel for Anna Lavinia to ride and showed her how to climb up into the saddle and where to scratch behind the camel's ears when she wanted him to kneel down. Next

the man tied her carpetbag on one side of the camel and the gardenia bush on the other.

The Pasha sleepily watched the camel being loaded, as he swatted at the flies with his curved sword. Just before Anna Lavinia was about to ride out of the palace, the Pasha cried out, "Bring her the talking parrot, so that she will have someone to talk to on the trip."

A servant brought in a lovely red and purple parrot and perched it on the camel's head, where it looked down at Anna Lavinia with a very proud look.

"Does it really talk?" Anna Lavinia asked, thinking of the doves at home that only sounded as though they were calling.

"It is just learning," the Pasha answered. "I have not taught it much yet, but it will repeat some things."

"Say something," Anna Lavinia said to the parrot.

The parrot looked at her proudly a moment and then said:

74

Twenty days has September,
April, Friday, and November.
The rest I really can't remember,
Save Monday alone,
Which is the longest day in the year.

"There, you see?" said the Pasha.

Anna Lavinia did not see. She thought the parrot had the words all wrong, and if it could do no better than that it ought to keep still. Yet she thought it would be rude to correct it just now, because perhaps it was the Pasha who did not have the words right. Therefore she thanked him and rode out of the pink palace and down the crooked street to the gate, thinking that her *Geography of the Desert* seemed to have left a few things out.

The Mirage

The Oasis

A R A

The Deep Forest

The Dark Tunnel

A MAP
That Shows
The Lay of the Land
Beyond
The Pawpaw Trees

The Village

B Y

The Pasha's Pink Palace

The Cliff

Where the Fat Woman got off the Train

Anna Lavinia's House

Chapter 7

An Island in the Sky

JUST as Anna Lavinia was going out the gate, glad to be on her way once more, the old man with the skinny finger stopped her, and she was afraid that he was going to try to get her to drink buttermilk after all. But instead he smiled a crooked smile and squeaked, "Beware of the mirages!"

Now, Anna Lavinia knew very well what mirages were, because she had read all about them in her geography, where they were all put down on a crinkling tissue-paper map, and her father had even marked one of them with an "X." They are supposed to be something you see that is not really there. Her mother said that it was just another proof of her rule that you should never believe what you see. But Anna Lavinia still thought that if you see a thing it must be there.

"How do you tell a mirage when you see one?" she asked the man with the skinny finger.

"Mirages," he said, wiggling his finger back and forth as he spoke, "usually float a little above the desert, and they wiggle a bit. When you ride up to them, they disappear. So no one has ever visited a mirage. But one of the best ways to find out whether what you see is a mirage or not is to take a thobby along. A thobby will no sooner go near a mirage than will a camel lead you to an empty well. They do not seem to believe in them, because they have no use for them, I suppose."

"What in the world is a thobby?" Anna Lavinia exclaimed.

The man with the skinny finger held out a box, about as big as a shoe box, and said, "There is a thobby in here, and you may take him with you."

Anna Lavinia took the box and lifted off the lid very carefully. The thobby looked up at her, blinking in the sun. Anna Lavinia stared in wonder. The thobby was a pretty sort of stubby-tailed lizard, very plump, about a foot long and covered with fur, mostly pink, but with round white spots.

"He won't bite, will he?" Anna Lavinia asked, shutting the box tight.

"Oh, no. Thobbies are very gentle, though stubborn," the man answered. "The Arab children all have them for pets instead of cats, since there are no mice in the desert."

"What shall I feed him?" Anna Lavinia asked, opening the box again just a little to have another peep.

"You don't have to feed him at all, because no one knows what thobbies eat," the man with the skinny finger replied.

Anna Lavinia thanked him and rode out the gate. After a little while she opened the box and let the thobby out. He hopped to the ground and trotted along after the camel, staying in the shadow so that his feet would keep cool.

Soon the walled town was out of sight. Far ahead of her in the distance Anna Lavinia could see what she knew was an oasis, and she headed her camel in that direction. It was very hot, and after the first hour the camel was not at all comfortable to ride. The hump was sharp, even through the padded saddle, and Anna Lavinia felt just like the train on the top of the hill, not sure whether she would slide forwards or backwards. It was really easier to walk beside the camel with the thobby and let Strawberry and the parrot ride.

The parrot kept repeating, "Twenty days has September," until Anna Lavinia was quite tired of it, and even Strawberry began to twitch his tail. So Anna Lavinia tried to teach the parrot one of Mrs. Tetterbrace's easiest songs:

The alphabet from A to Q
  Was all poor Suzy puzzled through,
Which really seems a sorry shame,
  Since she can never spell her name.

But Bab, who stopped with A and B,
  Can spell her name quite easily.
The lucky ones are those who get
  Names early in the alphabet.

All the parrot would learn was the first line, so Anna Lavinia gave up as they neared the oasis.

The oasis was small and not at all what she expected. There were only three palm trees and a patch of grass. There was also a well with a rope and a bucket, and Anna Lavinia hauled up water for the camel and Strawberry and the parrot. The thobby would not drink any.

All around the inside of the well were little steps cut into the rock so you could go down to the water, which was only about two feet deep. Anna Lavinia went down the steps and sat on the bottom one. It was delightfully cool, and she took off her shoes and stockings and waded in the water. A couple of yellow

frogs came out from a crack in the rocks to watch her, and the thobby flopped down the steps for a swim. When she was going up the steps again, Anna Lavinia noticed a small iron door in the side of the well, but it was locked tight and would not budge when she rattled it.

By now it was almost dark. The camel knelt down on the patch of grass and started to eat a cactus, wrinkling up his lips to avoid the thorns. Anna Lavinia took out the sandwiches her mother had made the day before and divided them with Strawberry. She gave the crusts of bread to the parrot, saying, "You might at least learn to say thank you."

The parrot looked up from the bread crumbs and answered, "You might at least learn September from A to Q."

Anna Lavinia laughed and decided that the Pasha had given her the parrot because it was too hard to teach it anything. Then she and Strawberry went to sleep under the plum-colored umbrella with the gold handle.

During the night it rained, and when she set out in the morning Anna Lavinia was over-joyed to see that all of the flowers that bloom in the desert when it rains, if it rains, were springing up all around. In the quiet of the desert she could hear the popping noise that the flower buds made when they burst open,

and she ran from one flower to another, de-lighted when she found one which her father had marked with an "X" in the geography. It must not have rained in a long time, because the thobby at first did not seem to know what to make of all the blossoms. He carefully sniffed at each one, and at last stuck out his long tongue to drink the honey out of them. So Anna Lavinia discovered that thobbies eat honey.

Before they had traveled far, Anna Lavinia saw what looked like a town ahead of them. Yet the more she looked at it, the surer she was that it was a mirage. There were palm trees and houses and tall towers with tops like onions just as there were in the town she visited the day before, but this time they all wiggled a little in the distance, as real mirages are supposed to do. As she came nearer, she noticed that the mirage did not rest on the ground. It seemed to float just a little above the surface of the desert. She could see clear underneath it, where it cast a rippling blue shadow on the sand.

Anna Lavinia shut her eyes tight and counted three before opening them. The mirage was still there. It did not go away at all as she approached. When she came quite close, she could see that it was floating gently about three feet off the ground. The wild flowers that grew on the edge hung over so that she could touch them, and when the camel began to nibble at some blue buttercups, Anna Lavinia knew she could believe what she saw.

The parrot hopped onto the mirage, saying, "You might at least learn to say thank you." Strawberry carefully walked up the camel's back and crawled onto the mirage too. The thobby alone did not seem willing to believe what he saw. Twice Anna Lavinia put him up on the edge of the mirage, and each time he purposely fell off again into the sand.

"This is getting tiresome," Anna Lavinia
finally said, and she took the thobby and shut
him up in the carpetbag. "Now, believe in
mirages or not, you're coming along." Then
she climbed onto the mirage herself and led
the camel up.

Only after they had traveled a good distance from the edge did Anna Lavinia let the thobby out of the carpetbag. Even then, to make sure that he would not fall through the floor of the mirage, she took from her pocket the piece of blue string with the silver key tied to it, and she knotted it around the thobby's neck. Every time the thobby started burrowing through the floor of the mirage, Strawberry would grab hold of the string and pull him back.

There was a cool breeze on the mirage that smelled of oranges and cinnamon, and the sky was a glorious lavender blue. As she approached the town at the center of the mirage, Anna Lavinia tried once again to teach the parrot a song. It must have been that the air was clearer, for the parrot learned the song quite easily, and it sang after Anna Lavinia:

Out beneath the lemon tree
Puss and I will take our tea.
Ginger cake and, just his size,
Little hot minced mouse-meat pies.

Later we will carve a melon—
Just for Puss's mice to dwell in.
Wait until the sunlight dies,
Fill a jar with fireflies.

When there's nothing else to do,
Maybe, then, we'll play with you.

The gates of the town stood open before her.

Chapter 8

The Musical Fountain

ANNA LAVINIA rode into the town. The very first person she asked said that, of course, her Aunt Sophia Maria lived there, pointing to a big square house in the main street. The house had no windows, but only a large pink door, where Anna Lavinia rang the shining brass bell.

She could hear the bell echoing all through the house, and in a moment the door opened and she knew the lady who answered was her Aunt Sophia Maria. Right away Anna Lavinia liked her. She had bright red hair and a pleasant smile, and she wore over her green dress a white apron with colored butterflies sewn on it.

Anna Lavinia did not need to tell her aunt who she was, for her aunt cried, "Anna Lavinia!" and she kissed her and took her into the house.

Then Anna Lavinia saw that the house did not need any windows on the outside, because almost all the inside was open to the sky. All

the rooms were arranged around a beautiful garden in the middle. The garden was filled with dozens of strange flowers and small fruit trees planted in patterns. In the very center stood a musical fountain. It was covered with hanging silver bells of all sizes that played a tune as the water spurted over them. Finally the water tumbled into a quiet wading pool filled with blue water lilies and silvery goldfish. Her Aunt Sophia Maria took Anna Lavinia upstairs to her bedroom, where there was a balcony hanging over the garden, and pink and white striped roses were twisted all about the railing.

The very first thing Anna Lavinia did when she had unpacked was to give her aunt the gardenia bush and the three jars of pawpaw jelly she had left. She was very glad to be rid of them at last. The gardenia bush had grown so fast in the desert air that it was much too big for the pot it was in, and her aunt took a spade and planted it in the garden right away, being careful not to dig too deep. Later Anna Lavinia asked her aunt where she could keep her animals, and her aunt said that she would have the camel put in a pasture near the house. The thobby could play in the garden and drink honey from the flowers. The parrot would stay in the dining room, where her aunt had two parrots of her own, so they could talk together and improve their vocabularies. Strawberry, of course, could go wherever he pleased, so long as he did not bother the goldfish.

After lunch, her aunt took Anna Lavinia upstairs and told her that since she was in Arab country she should have proper clothes to wear. Opening a sandalwood chest, her Aunt Sophia Maria took out three of the silk nightgown sort of dresses Anna Lavinia admired so much and a pair of green leather shoes with curled toes and half a dozen strings of sparkling beads.

Anna Lavinia spent most of the rest of the day trying on her new clothes or playing in the garden with Strawberry and the thobby, tasting each of the curious fruits, while her Aunt Sophia Maria played at the piano and sang all the songs from Mrs. Tetterbrace's *Songs from Nowhere*. Anna Lavinia had never heard them played on a piano before, since her own piano at home had most of the strings broken. Together they sang the round,

which Anna Lavinia had not bothered to learn
because it takes two to sing it:

> If I were you,
> And you were me,
> I cannot tell
> What I would be.
>
> But I can tell you,
> Quick as fleas,
> I think that you'd
> Be bound to please.

Anna Lavinia was surprised that her aunt knew all the songs, but when she remarked about it, her Aunt Sophia Maria chuckled and whispered in Anna Lavinia's ear. Then she opened an old wooden cupboard full of books all alike, and she gave Anna Lavinia a brand-new copy of the songs.

When it got dark, her aunt strung green and yellow paper lanterns all around the garden, and they had dinner beside the fountain with candles on the table. Almost all the food had whipped cream on it, for her Aunt Sophia Maria told Anna Lavinia, "If a thing is good, it is always better with whipped cream." And it was.

Finally Anna Lavinia got so sleepy that her aunt carried her up to bed. As her aunt was tucking her in, the musical fountain bubbling in the center of the garden began to play a sleepy tune, and her aunt sang the words:

Come out! Come out! The night is cool,
    The stars are swinging in the sky.
Across the rippled garden pool,
    The moon spills silver down from high.

Then leave the house, and come with me
    Where rabbits run on silent paws
Through dew-wet fields, where we may see
    Night beetles wash their amber claws.

Come, where ferns and harebells grow,
    And the earth smells sweet and good.
Listen! Strange, and sad, and slow,
    Owl calls to owl across the wood.

There may have been more to the song, but Anna Lavinia was so pleasantly drowsy that she did not hear the rest.

Chapter 9

A Song from Now Here

WHILE Anna Lavinia was dressing the next morning, she kept waiting to hear a mopstick thumped on the floor, but instead her Aunt Sophia Maria tapped softly at her door, bringing her a cup of hot cocoa with whipped cream on it, and a dish of whipped cream for Strawberry, who got it all over his whiskers.

"Anna Lavinia," her aunt said, "you must try the echo from your balcony. It is always best in the morning when the air is still."

Therefore Anna Lavinia stepped out onto the balcony, where the pink and white striped roses were still wet with dew, and she called, "Echo!"

At once the echo answered, "Echo!"

"Try something else, Anna Lavinia," her aunt said.

So Anna Lavinia sang out the first two lines of one of the *Songs from Nowhere*:

> The Spangled Pandemonium
> Is missing from the zoo.

Anna Lavinia waited for the lines to be repeated, but instead the echo answered with the next two lines of the song:

> He bent the bars the barest bit,
> And slithered glibly through.

This was the most peculiar echo Anna Lavinia had ever heard, and she turned around to see if her Aunt Sophia Maria might not be having something to do with it. After all, she knew the song too. But she was standing right beside Anna Lavinia, looking just as much surprised. So Anna Lavinia continued with the next four lines of the song, all in one breath as fast as she could to confuse the echo:

99

He crawled across the moated wall,
He climbed the mango tree,
And when his keeper scrambled up,
He nipped him in the knee.

But, just as quickly, the echo answered, all
in one breath:

To all of you, a warning
Not to wander after dark,
Or if you must, make very sure
You stay out of the park.

For the Spangled Pandemonium
Is missing from the zoo,
And since he nipped his keeper,
He would just as soon nip you!

While the echo was answering with the
rest of the song, Anna Lavinia tried to hear
exactly where the sound was coming from,
and it sounded as though it were just beneath
her in the garden, where the sunlight coming
across the orange tiles of the roof made a sort

of rainbow in the fine spray of the fountain. Leaning over the railing as far as she dared, Anna Lavinia peered down. Standing there under the balcony, looking up at her with a twinkle in his eye, stood her father!

For the first time in her life, Anna Lavinia could hardly believe what she saw. So she shut her eyes, quickly counted three, and then opened them again. Yes, her father was really there, wearing the same old mustard-colored trousers and bottle-green jacket with the pocket microscope bulging in one pocket and a gray goose feather sticking out of the other.

Anna Lavinia could not get down the stairs fast enough. All the way down her heart was in her mouth, for fear her father might see the rainbow in the fountain and be gone before she reached him, and she was very careful where she stepped on the pattern of the stair carpet. But her father was right there at the foot of the stairs, and he snatched her up and whirled her three times round his head before he hugged her and set her down. He looked just as she remembered him, only his red beard was even longer and ticklier.

After a little while Anna Lavinia asked him to take out his pocket microscope to show her some motes in the sunbeams, because she had been waiting so long to see them, and they looked exactly like stars or snowflakes, only they were gold.

"Real gold?" Anna Lavinia asked.

"Some of them," her father answered, "but mostly fool's gold."

Her father had so many questions to ask Anna Lavinia about herself and her mother that it was a long time before Anna Lavinia could get him to talk about himself. He told her that he would have been home much sooner, except that he had lost something and had been spending most of his time in the desert with a sieve, sifting the sand to find it.

"Whatever was it you were looking for?" Anna Lavinia asked.

"A little silver key, but I have not found it yet," he said, and he burst out singing the very last of the *Songs from Nowhere*:

When I was young and full of hope,
    I braided me a length of rope,
To tie about the bag of gold
    That I would have when I was old.

Now, old and poor, I've lost my hope,
    But still I have that piece of rope,
Which I will carry, though I'm told
    The rope's no good without the gold.

When her father finished singing, he looked very sad. Anna Lavinia, on the other hand, at once remembered the key which the man with the vegetable cart had given her, and she was filled with joy to think that she would be able to help her father.

"Was it," Anna Lavinia asked, "a very small silver key tied to a piece of blue string?"

Her father's face lit up. "That is the very one. Where did you see it, Anna Lavinia?"

Anna Lavinia beamed. "I have it right here," she said, reaching in her pocket.

Suddenly she felt queer all over. The key was gone. When she had tied the string around the thobby's neck she had forgotten to take off the key.

Anna Lavinia ran to look for the thobby, searching high and low for him in the garden and all through the house, but he was nowhere to be found. Anna Lavinia even looked in her carpetbag, while her Aunt Sophia Maria splashed about in the fountain with a net. At last Anna Lavinia found a hole in the garden near the gardenia bush, and the footprints of the thobby were all around it. When her father poked in the hole with a stick, they could see daylight through the hole and the desert beneath, but no thobby.

Anna Lavinia burst into tears. It was all her fault, and she knew she should never have taken that key out of her pocket.

Chapter 10

Heard in a Sea Shell

"COME, come. There's no use crying, my dappled duck," her father said to Anna Lavinia, adding that thobbies can never be trusted on mirages. "If we hurry, we may be able to catch up with him. But we must go at once."

While her Aunt Sophia Maria ran to get the camel from the pasture, Anna Lavinia quickly folded her new dresses into the carpetbag and tucked in her new copy of the *Songs from Nowhere*. The camel was soon ready and the carpetbag tied on and the parrot perched on the camel's head and Strawberry in the saddle.

The very last minute, the parrot shrieked out, "You might at least learn to say thank you." Anna Lavinia quickly thanked her aunt, and they set out.

At the edge of the mirage, they found that it had risen a few feet since the day before, so that it was quite a jump for the camel, but he made it all right. Anna Lavinia could not help thinking that it must have been a jolt for the poor thobby, but her father said that maybe it would shake some sense into him.

In no time at all Anna Lavinia and her father reached the oasis with the three palm trees. When Anna Lavinia went down the steps in the well to cool her feet, there, swimming in the bottom, looking very much ashamed, was the thobby, with the key still around his neck.

Anna Lavinia's father gave a whoop of joy, and taking the key he dashed up the stone steps to the little iron door. He thrust the key in and turned it four times to the right and three times to the left, and the little door swung open. Inside, on the damp stone floor, were fourteen small iron pots all full of gold.

"Real gold?" Anna Lavinia asked, wanting to be sure.

"Real gold," her father answered, clinking together a couple of pieces in his hand.

"Is it all yours?" Anna Lavinia asked again.

"All ours," her father replied. "This is the gold that you find at the end of the rainbow."

At last Anna Lavinia knew why her father was always chasing rainbows, and she felt sure that her mother would feel better about it when she knew too.

After they had rested at the oasis awhile, Anna Lavinia and her father put the gold into the carpetbag, and they rode off to the high cliff. Her father said he hoped Anna Lavinia would be able to climb up all right, although it was pretty steep, and might take a day or two.

Anna Lavinia had no idea of climbing up at all. "Everything that comes down must go up," she said, and she picked up a stone and tossed it into the air. Very slowly, much more slowly than it had come down, the stone began to rise, until it was out of sight. Next she picked up Strawberry and gave him a gentle shove upwards. He too began to sail up.

Anna Lavinia's father was amazed. "I don't know why I never thought of that before," he said. "To think of all the times I've climbed up and down that cliff!"

"It takes a little pushing," Anna Lavinia answered. She was very proud of herself, even though she had not been at all sure that it would really work.

Because the carpetbag was full of gold, it took a great deal of pushing, but eventually it started up. The camel was much more of a problem. Anna Lavinia and her father, both pushing together, could not get him to budge.

Anna Lavinia considered the problem a moment. "Perhaps the umbrella would help," she said, remembering how it had slowed her coming down the cliff.

Therefore they opened her plum-colored umbrella and tied the gold handle to the saddle and then gave the camel another shove. At last the camel began to rise, paddling his long legs in the air as he lumbered into the sky.

The thobby, on the other hand, would not go up at all. Anna Lavinia had to carry him, since the carpetbag was already gone, and he wiggled stubbornly all the way. Only the parrot needed no pushing. Anna Lavinia said to it, "You can fly, if you want to," and all the way up the parrot screamed, "You can fly if you want to," as it passed Anna Lavinia and

her father and the camel and Strawberry. As
they neared the top, they could see the fat
woman's tea cosy still floating in the warm
air, where it had been all the time. Anna
Lavinia snatched it as she went past. "You
never know when you might need a tea cosy,"
the fat woman had said.

The train was standing exactly where Anna Lavinia had left it. It looked just the same, except that the green onions, which Anna Lavinia had tucked under one of the seats, had begun to grow, and the leaves hung out of the windows of the coach. Anna Lavinia's father poked about the machinery for a long time. Finally he got the engine started.

"Do you think the wheels will ever straighten out?" Anna Lavinia asked him.

"As soon as the train moves a little, the tracks ought to push the wheels back in place," her father answered. "But since there is no way of turning the train around, we will have to go backwards all the way."

"Well, we want to go backwards anyway," Anna Lavinia laughed. She certainly did not want to go forwards over the cliff. There might be a limit to what would go down gently. So, on the back of the sign reading, "END OF THE LINE," Anna Lavinia carefully spelled out, with a piece of chalky stone, the three words, "THIS WAY BACK."

As the engine began to work, the steam whistled out and the whole train shook. Anna Lavinia and her father hurried to put everything into the coach. The camel got in all right, but his head stuck out one of the windows. Anna Lavinia tied the tea cosy around his ears so that he would not catch cold. The thobby and Strawberry and the parrot each took a separate seat, so they could see the view. Once they got started, Anna Lavinia's father came and sat beside her. After all, the train ran very well without anyone at the engine.

The trip going back was exactly like the trip going forwards, except that it was backwards. Somewhere in the dark forest they

found the engineer, with his mustache all curly from the rain, walking along the tracks carrying a lantern, looking for the train, and they took him aboard. At the station where the fat woman had gotten off, she got on again. She had sold all her tea cosies, and Anna Lavinia was happy to see her and to thank her for the package she had left her.

Strawberry had to be squeezed into the carpetbag once more, but the fat woman fell in love with the thobby, especially when she learned that he liked sweets, and she held him in her lap, feeding him honey cakes, until Anna Lavinia and her father reached their station.

Shortly before they arrived, the parrot surprised them all by bursting out singing a strange new song, which Anna Lavinia supposed it must have learned from her Aunt Sophia Maria's parrots:

Heard in a Sea Shell

In Babylon bright gardens hung
Halfway to heaven, where there swung
Silk tasseled ladders, letting down
To those who went up from the town,
To gibble and to gabble on
The hanging walls of Babylon.

There, gentlemen and ladies
Of the Tigris or Euphrates
Found it pleasing to meander
Through green groves of oleander,
Jasmine, rose, and asphodel,
Till each painted petal fell.

Till, with breaking of the spell,
Halfway heaven heaved and rumbled,
Each silk tasseled ladder tumbled,
Each bright hanging garden crumbled,
And the lazy scented day
    Passed away.

"How foolish!" exclaimed the fat woman,
as she petted the smiling thobby in her lap.

"Picture a garden hanging without anything to hold it up! I'll never believe that could be."

Thinking that a silk tasseled ladder would have come in handy on the mirage, Anna Lavinia had her mouth all open to explain to the fat woman just how that could be, when she saw her father wink at her, touching a finger to his lips. She thought a moment and then knew why. If, like the thobby, a person has already made up his mind not to believe a thing, no amount of talking in the world will do any good.

When they got off the train at last, they happened to meet the man with the vegetable cart, and Anna Lavinia's father reached into the carpetbag and gave him a piece of rainbow gold for having taken such good care of his key. Then they slowly began walking through the village up the long hill home. It was still very early in the morning, and all the people in the village ran to their windows in their nightgowns to see Anna Lavinia leading her camel with the parrot perched on his

head and Strawberry riding in the saddle and the thobby trotting behind in the shadow.

As they came to their house and opened the gate, they could smell the pawpaw jelly cooking in the kitchen. Looking up, Anna Lavinia saw that the sky was lavender blue, just as she always knew it would be on the day her father came home. The parrot flew into a pawpaw tree and began singing everything it knew. The thobby, after first testing the ground to make sure that it could not burrow through, headed for a petunia bed to eat honey. Strawberry went to his favorite tree and began to sharpen his claws, which were pretty dull from walking in the desert.

Stopping at the well, Anna Lavinia prodded the hedgehog gently with the point of her plum-colored umbrella, and when it opened its eyes, she leaned down and winked at it. Reaching into her pocket, Anna Lavinia took out her handkerchief and carefully unwrapped a prickly pear from her Aunt Sophia Maria's garden, and she placed it gingerly just at the entrance to the hedgehog's nest. In one of the pawpaw trees a dove called, "Who knows now? Who? who? who?" and somewhere beyond the pawpaw trees another dove answered: "You know now! You! you! you!" Just what she was supposed to know now Anna Lavinia could not be sure, for her mind was full of a great many things, and like peppermint in the mouth, they were still too close. But she did know now that the tingling feeling, like the taste of peppermint, would last for a long time.

Her father told her to go on ahead into the house while he unloaded the camel. So she ran round to the front door and into the kitchen, where her mother was standing at the stove, stirring a huge kettle of pawpaw jelly and singing the old half-forgotten song about the sea shell.

"Help yourself to oatmeal, dear," she said to Anna Lavinia, too busy to look up from her stirring.

Anna Lavinia took two dishes and put oatmeal in them, and then buried a big lump of butter in each.

Her mother watched her out of the corner of her eye. "What are you doing with two dishes? I've had my oatmeal already," she said.

"But my father will want his too," Anna Lavinia answered, trying hard not to laugh, because she knew perfectly well what her mother would answer.

The answer came. Clapping her wooden spoon on the kettle with each word, her mother said, "Your father is chasing rain-bows."

But, before she could begin to cry as she usually did, there was a dreadful clatter at the back door as it swung open, upsetting jar after jar of pawpaw jelly, and Anna Lavinia's father stepped through the pantry into the kitchen, with the fourteen pots of gold all piled one on top of the other.

"And at last he has found his rainbows!" he said.

Anna Lavinia's mother was so happy to see him that she did not know whether to laugh or to cry, so she did both, and Anna

Lavinia handed her the fat woman's tea cosy to wipe her eyes.

"What a lovely tea cosy!" her mother exclaimed. "It is just like the one my mother had when I was a little girl." Suddenly her mother's face grew strangely bright. "My song!" she cried. "Seeing the tea cosy has made me remember it!"

All the tired look went out of her mother's eyes, and Anna Lavinia thought her mother seemed almost a child again herself, as she leaned down towards Anna Lavinia and sang, very softly:

I held a sea shell to my ear,
   Because they told me I would hear
The magic song the mermaids sing,
   The rush of waves along the shore.

And though I listened, oh, so long!
   Yet never heard one note of song,
To me it was a magic thing:
   That hush of silence—nothing more!

Her mother paused a moment, as if still not quite remembering the words, so Anna Lavinia's father put his arm around her mother's shoulder, and together her mother and father sang the rest:

> Far stranger than a chanted spell,
> > Far stronger than the ocean's swell,
> That silence, like a hidden spring,
> > Half opened heaven's highest door.

Then, because she saw that Anna Lavinia was about to cry too, her mother put down the tea cosy, which she had been holding to her ear as if it were a sea shell. Clapping her ladle against the jelly kettle, she said, "Anna Lavinia, your spoon is sticking straight up in your oatmeal again, like a palm tree on an oasis!"

And, sure enough, it was.

The End

PALMER BROWN was born in Chicago and attended Swarthmore and the University of Pennsylvania. He is the author and illustrator of five books for children, including *Beyond the Pawpaw Trees* and its sequel, *The Silver Nutmeg*; *Cheerful*; and *Hickory*. About *Beyond the Pawpaw Trees*, his first published book, Brown said: "If it has any moral at all, it is hoped that it will always be a deep secret between the author and those of his readers who still know that believing is seeing."

ELEANOR FARJEON
The Little Bookroom

PENELOPE FARMER
Charlotte Sometimes

RUMER GODDEN
An Episode of Sparrows
The Mousewife

LUCRETIA P. HALE
The Peterkin Papers

RUSSELL and LILLIAN HOBAN
The Sorely Trying Day

RUTH KRAUSS and MARC SIMONT
The Backward Day

MUNRO LEAF and ROBERT LAWSON
Wee Gillis

RHODA LEVINE and EDWARD GOREY
Three Ladies Beside the Sea

NORMAN LINDSAY
The Magic Pudding

ERIC LINKLATER
The Wind on the Moon

J. P. MARTIN
Uncle
Uncle Cleans Up

JOHN MASEFIELD
The Box of Delights
The Midnight Folk

E. NESBIT
The House of Arden

DANIEL PINKWATER
Lizard Music

ALASTAIR REID and BOB GILL
Supposing…

ALASTAIR REID and BEN SHAHN
Ounce Dice Trice

BARBARA SLEIGH
Carbonel and Calidor
Carbonel: The King of the Cats
The Kingdom of Carbonel

E. C. SPYKMAN
Terrible, Horrible Edie

FRANK TASHLIN
The Bear That Wasn't

JAMES THURBER
The 13 Clocks
The Wonderful O

ALISON UTTLEY
A Traveller in Time

T. H. WHITE
Mistress Masham's Repose

MARJORIE WINSLOW and ERIK BLEGVAD
Mud Pies and Other Recipes

REINER ZIMNIK
The Bear and the People